Life Love Experience

Poems from the heart

By

Peinsejoager

Life Love Experience
Copyright © 2020 Peinsejoager
Published by FDW Consulting
All rights reserved

Cover design by: Peinsejoager

ISBN-13: 978-87-972426-0-5
ISBN-10: 87-972426-0-8

For all people,
Passing through,
Living life,
Finding love,
Experiencing...

____

CONTENTS

Opening

This bundle takes you on a journey in the form of scribblings that some people might refer to as poems. These are poems written from the heart and have helped the author come to terms with certain realities in life, in love and in experiencing.

We all feel. At any time when we live our lives, when we fall in love, when we love, when we walk our path and when we journey into the unknown, we experience by feeling. The verses in this bundle are snapshots that deal with such feelings and are an attempt to understand how we absorb them into ourselves to make them part of our being.

Each word, sentence and verse has meaning and expresses a state of sensing and conveys emotions that results into feeling, however flawed the words may be...

01

Life

Question!

15

Primitive writing suggests the primitive,
Does the primitive suggest primitive writing?
Or, are we just talking in code?

?

Distance

Distance develops longing
Longing defines our desire

And when we meet again

Closeness triggers passion
Passion defines our love

And when we stay together

Unity captures happiness
Happiness defines our life...

Coming Home

Hours pass by...
Days gone by...
Mentally worn,
But peace of mind found
With a bleeding heart,
And a mind torn.

Pieces come together,
Jigsaws to be matched
Love is found, never lost

Time was needed,
to heal this pain...
Time was required,
to correct the path

Help still required,
from you, my love

Help still needed,
by you, my friend

Help is welcomed
by you, my beloved

Help is accepted,
from you, my life

Question! (Variant)

Primitive writing suggests the complex,
Does the complex require primitive writing?
Or, are we just talking in code?

Existence

Days pass by, thoughtful about the end of a time,
Where joy is concealed and pain is oppressed
and our hearts meet in the present
Surrounded by uncertainty
Where things are certain, but not mentioned or told
and our lives twisted by gold.

Trust in this dream
Hold on to your soul,
So long... I see you fade
Holding on, every day
So long... I feel you fade
Holding on to this dream

Weeks pass by, thinking about the beginning of time,
where life is created and seeds are planted
and our hearts meet in that place
surrounded by goodness
where things are certain, but uncertain in time
and our lives entangled by our hearts

Believe in your dreams
Hold on to your soul
So long... I see you fade
Holding on. each day
So long... I feel you fade
Holding on to this reality

Months pass by, thinking about what has been,
Where love is felt and friendship grew
and our hearts intertwine
surrounded by wonder
where things are certain, eternal and timeless
and our lives connected by love

Rise above those dreams
Hold on to your soul
So long... I see you fade
Holding on, every day
So long... I feel you fade
Holding on to this truth

Years pass by, thinking about what is to come
Where affection is present and emotions real
and hearts still pounding with love
surrounded by trust
where things are infinite, moving and in motion
and our lives locked by our bond

Rise above this vision
Hold on to your soul
So long... I see us fade
Holding on, every day
So long... I feel us fade
Believing in our strength

Decades pass by, thinking about what is and was
where reflection influences thoughts
and feelings of control fade
surrounded by a sense of sadness
where people vanish, entering a state of loneliness
and life is at an end

Rise above this perception
Hold on to your beliefs
So long... I see the end
Letting go, for a split second
So long... I feel peace
Entering a new existence

Centuries pass by, dust is what should be
Where existence is existential
and hearts do not exist
surrounded by perception
where everything is ethereal, fading in time
and life is eternal

ᴐ ᴐ ᴐ

The Storyteller

A story is told,
The whisperer accounts,

About the struggle
for liberty and freedom
for brotherhood and unity

The telling of tales,
About shedding the shackles of ignorance...

An Observation

When you treat friends like adversaries,
And allies like enemies...
What is left to do with your enemies?
Befriend them to avoid serious conflict?

Let us hope wisdom prevails,
And disagreement is overcome by sanity...
What other expectations should we have?
Allowing egos rampage the stage?

A Story Of...

Oh, why this feeling, again
It was something of the past
Never to appear again,
So, I thought...

Spikes are back in the head,
A constant state of pain
Commencing at the break of dawn,
So, I sense...

Is it worry?
Is it strain?
Or just another chapter in this game?

Must hold on
To the small things that matter,
Must be thankful
For what you receive and have,
Cherish and respect
To those close to you and care,

My heart,
belongs to you
My wealth,
is my love for you

While you calm my spirit with your kisses
And ease the discomfort with your touch
I search for the source
Hidden in the depths of my soul...

Purpose

Walk the path of life
No matter that you believe and have faith
Or use reason and think

Straight roads you expect await
Instead, bumps and bends are confronted
Concrete walls cemented

No compromise in their thoughts
No heart in their decisions
No empathy in their actions

Saving was the goal
Cold calculated directions given
Affecting people in their hearts,
Destroying loyalty and engagement
A purpose of existence scratched,
Without the slightest consideration

Walk the path of life
Believe in yourself,
Have faith in people that care

Walk the path of life
Use reason as your guide
Think, use your brain as your conscious

While licking wounds and getting back on your feet
With help and support of your loved ones
Think of this, for a brief moment,
That hope peeks around the corner, constantly

Reconnecting to a purpose of life
Encrypted in feelings and perception
Decrypt it with passion and devotion
Let it be driven by love and friendship

The Mirror

I saw a mirror looking at me,
No reflection
The saddest image I've ever seen,
Seeking redemption

Tough Memories

Looking out the window
A vast space in front of me
Thinking back when pain was felt
And fear was ever present
Remembering times of loneliness

Crawling into my soul
A dark place to be, not free
Reflecting on that night, a long time ago
Being in dismay and pain
Waking up in a foreign place

Staring into a void
A distance, far away
Meditating, searching for some peace
An effort to make sense of it all
Accepting, at least trying... for now

Glancing at a beam of light
A glimpse of hope
Listening to your voice
Leading me down the path,
Finding purpose and strength

Evolution

(2 Verses on Transcendence)

Deep feelings track the mind
Following intuition,
Passing by a sign...
Following impulse,
Acting by instinct...
Following a hunch,
Moving slowly closer...

Am I making progress?
Moving beyond that place,
Surpassing the current world,
Ascending into a new state,
Advancing slowly,
Transcending beyond my imagination...

A Tormented Soul

A composition of being
- Out of Balance -

I.

For a moment there,
I thought all was well.
Then came the shock,
And all became dark again

A realisation of hurt
A nightmare resurrected
Out of the ashes of the past
Comes a monster from within

Finding peace is all I want
Being me is what I crave
Being you is what I loath
Finding harmony is all I need

Every day my head explodes
Seeking the dark, avoiding light
No antidote, no cure in sight
Every day I walk this road

II.

Three Critical Junctures

1989

Attacked by a mob
Abrupt ending of a dream
Waking up in despair
Long road to recover
Soul tormented by fear
Mind broken, shattered
A life in solitude
Walking the path to repair

1996

Decisions made,
Leaving it all behind,
Reborn in strength
Self-conscious, confident

Body and Soul
In harmony at last
Will and resolve
aligned in unity

2017

Confidence shattered
Pain erupted
Old wounds opened
unexpected, unprepared

Mirrors show others
Looking at them
Afraid of the reflections
Fighting hard to get control

∧

III.

Accept new reality
Do not dwell in the past
Dealing with inner demons
Taking the path ahead

Find Inner Peace
Strengthen the mind
Trust the ones who care
Let them embrace your heart

Thinking Positive
Guided by my values
I walk this path of healing
Knowing I am not left on my own

∧

IV.

Making efforts to push away the pain...

Peace

Can I have some solitude, please
Just for some days
Can I find some peace, please
Fighting the pain inside
Can I ask for your trust, please
Undeserved but sincere,
To hide from the light...

I need the space
I need the tranquility
I need the meditation
I need the peace

Needed it yesterday,
Need it today,
And certainly,
Need it tomorrow....

Communication

In a time of change
Syllables clash with one another
Debating the meaning of existence

In a time of extremes
Bits and bytes transmit to one another
Influencing the meaning of debate

While sometime later...

A crowd floods the streets
Shouting out in protest
Against oppressive forces
Signaling the time of reckoning

Hashtag

Fear to become a hashtag #fear
Ambition to be a hashtag #ambition
Fame through a hashtag #fame

Your existence #myexistence
Your life #mylife
Your values #myvalues
Your world #myworld

All reduced to a hashtag #I_exist

02

Love

For a Brief Moment...

For a brief moment I saw you sitting there
Looking at my soul
Touching the source of my pain
Exiling its existence,
Making room
For peace and unity...

Two Hearts

Wandering
Into an abyss
Finding comfort

Two hearts
Beating
Boom Boom Boom

Connecting
In the inner circle
Finding darkness

Two hearts
Competing
Boom Boom Boom

Walking
Down a path
Finding you

Two hearts
Embracing
Boom Boom Boom

Reaching
For your hands
Finding safety

Two hearts
Entwine
Boom Boom Boom

A Sparkle of...

Can we design our dreams?
Express our thoughts...
(Never to get lost)

Should we submit to hope?
For a modest moment
For pain to dissolve
(Some might say submit to faith)

Can we build that future?
With passion, fulfilling our desires
While being loved,
With heart and soul, grateful to the bone

Experience kindness, a feeling of empathy,
An act with dignity...
(So grateful you are here)
Appease, looking for peace,
Embracing your presence
(Casting eyes to the future)

I am shedding that pain, trying to...
(Some day) ... (Soon)
Dropping these shackles,
(Fulfilling our destiny of some kind...)
To be released from this torment,

We shall stay true,
Committed to life... Together...

Sweet Love

Watching the colors fade,
Transforming into black and white.

A playful silhouette emerging the scene,
Provoking my senses, touching my feelings.

My heart and my soul surrender,
When you lay in my arms.

While I am fading away in sweet dreams,
Eyes closed embracing you through this night...

Eternity

For my Ice Queen,
When shivering cold takes hold of your body
For my Hot Thing,
When heat chases away that cold
I feel you close to me,
While your breath travels over my skin
I feel your touch,
While my love is set for eternity

For

For you,
Thoughts of love emerge,
At every moment of the day,
Seeing you smile and those eyes glimpse over to me

For me,
Feelings of love emerge,
Every evening, hugging on the path,
Feeling your body against mine expressing care

For us,
Feeling affection with each gentle touch
Every day, we snuggle and hold
Caress the tenderness that fills the sheets

Dance of Love

A breath of air,
Gently
Passes by your ear.
You make a sound,
Approving
Of warm air touching

A slight touch,
Caring
On your shoulder.
You breath, in and out,
Intense
Absorbing the touch

Fingers move up and down,
Playful
Touching your arm
You answer,
Frolic
Teasing my hand

A loving kiss,
Softly
In your neck.
Your lips reach out
Willfully
Embracing a passionate kiss

A touch on your back,
Wanting
Playing with your senses.
You move your leg over mine,
Signaling
We do the dance of love

Strong Emotions

A slight breeze touches the skin
Hot evening, passion erupts from within
Thoughts develop, motion at play
Where love is movement away

Yearning for that moment
Once more,
Where affection turns to lust
And lust transforms to passion

Writing that song of love,
Reciting that lost poem
Full of affection, deep in the heart
While dreaming of a continued future
Side by side, united as one...

There is

There is no doubt
Never was and never will be

There is some fear
The path to take is never certain

There is no hesitation
The feelings are true and clear

There might be confusion
Some things will clear in time

There is no distrust
Soulmates for life, right

There is pain
Yes, it hurts both ways

There is love
Unconditioned and more

There is friendship
Honest and pure

There is us
United and more...

Forbidden Fruit

Longing for something that does not exist,
While the heart pounds,
Deep inside this body, a feeling of lust resides
Wanting to break out,
When bodies finally touch, surrendering
Giving every way they want

Huh... What?

our fantasies are intriguing me
your thoughts are arousing me

my fantasies are locked away
my thoughts are just not for play

I see
I feel
I long
I play

Where is your touch? Will it come?
Will it stay?

Valentine

Cupid struck, a long time ago
An arrow in the heart
Stunned by the blow

From that moment I knew,
That you would be mine
And forever be,
My valentine

A Mental State

A statement from the heart,
No exit! No entry! Stop!
Stuck in a bubble... no room for rewind...
Only one way to go, forward I guess.
Will you be there?

Closing eyes to catch a glimpse,
Emotional wrecks, we both are
I sure hope you will be there
Finding solace in each other's arms.

Hurting

Why do we hurt the ones we love most?
Words of apologies should flood the gates,
Yet I have nothing to say...

Feelings of embarrassment, for sure...
Walking in a void, lost
Abandoned myself, forlorn...

Feelings of sadness, mostly that...
Oh yes, it is my own doing
Trapped in myself, loneliness...

How do we find trust again?
When suspicion is ever present...
How do I come back to sanity?
While I drown in gloomy emotions...

Only with you, my dear...
Only together...
Only us...

Where

Where feelings meet
and emotions great

Where passion is found
and love is bound

Where friendship arose
and relationship grows

Where do we go...?

Where perception composes
a cocktail of desire

Where feelings deliver
a thrill and vibe

Where our hearts
come together as one

Where do we go...?

Where we overcome
the pain and chaos of longing

Where we find
those moments of milk and honey

Where do we go...?

That place where we are,
Together for always...

Love

The scent of a morning brew
Penetrates the senses,
Submitting to fantasies of lust
Wishing to explore,
Those boundaries of love

So longing for your touch,
Right now,
A desire to experience your passion

The thought of your kisses,
Covering my neck, my body
Take me to places,
Beyond my wildest dreams,
Making me to want you...

Making love to you
Until the end of days

Dance of Love II

One night,
not so long ago

A soft gentle touch,
Lights a spark, a trigger for
A twinkling feeling of desire
Oh, It has been so long...

While moving a little closer,
The sound of rain crackles down the window

A little later,
Fingertips brushing your inner thigh
Waiting for consent
Listening for a sound,
A slight moan to be released,
Inviting...
Calling out for more, a soft feeling
Arms move tighter,
Holding firmer, rocking our bodies slow...

The feeling of soft kisses,
So gently and real,
Experiencing deep affection
Dancing the dance of love...

03

Experience

A Bubble

Calming soothing dreams
Horrid painful screams
Join me in my dreams
Abandoning those screams

The Sleeper

Sinking deeper
Wake up the sleeper
Syncing realities
Erase the fantasies

Searching

Calling for you,
Deep down there,
In the corner of that soul,
Sensing the pain,
and the grief,
A bleeding heart,
That does not leave stains in the snow
Buried deep,
Where it feels,
You are not in control of your thoughts anymore

Go away... Leave me alone... PAIN
Stay out of my head... PAIN
You are not welcome anymore... PAIN

"Who would have thought you would try to get back in
control?"

I am here... Fighting...
.... PAIN ....
Battling the pain away, igniting the fire...

"Who are you to think... (??)"

My thoughts are mine!
My feelings are mine!

Somewhere there is an end point,
Take my hand,
Guide me through this (   )
Hold me in your arms,
Safe to be here,
Protected from (   )
Somewhere there is a starting point...

)

A Good Day

Walking through the narrow streets
The sun peaks through the clouds
We venture into this new place
A first impression, full of joy
Experiencing as always, together
It is a good day...

Small houses and cobble stones
A romantic setting, for a joyful day
We walk hand in hand
A cozy feeling, full of warmth
Small coffee house serving,
It is a good day...

Afternoon chill, a slight breeze
while walking through the street
finding a new destination
Sitting down at a corner cafe
Cool beer served, nuts on the side
It is a good day...

Evening setting in,
A drizzle cannot kill the mood
Diner time, a feast served
Bit by bit, enjoying every detail of this moment
Experiencing as we always do, together
It is a good day...

☾

Clouds

So long, my dear
For the time is near,
Where we live in fear
And see loved ones,
March to disappear

Good Bye, peace
Is it too late?
Or just not yet,
That hope still is embraced
to find some happiness

Warmongers create fear
and divide to conquer
Call names to provoke
Send armies to destroy and plunder
Until there is nothing left

Hello, my dear
I hold you near
and I have no fear
For our love is strong
And ever so real

I embrace, our love
finding warmth and care
in this cold hard world
You and me and us
Together, in the hope it all will be better

Oh, so afraid...
Mushroom clouds are not welcome
Not here nor in my nightmares
Friendship and love are found
when people talk and listen

Understand cultural differences
Embrace our diversity
and learn from one another
To embrace a prosperous life
As equals under the same sky

Not damaged by clouds

Cry Out

Collapsing into madness,
Brain damage? Heart shattered...
All confidence is broken,
So far away those dreams are

Each little feeling
Expanding into eternal
Experiencing as deep pain...

Where am I? Can I ask?
Who is this? Should I ask?

So far, no answer... Yet!
Condemned to solitude,

So, we think,
Crawling into defense,

So, we shrink
Holding on to the signs

With exponential feelings of regret,
Ending the days in emotional debt...

Is There Hope?

A sudden feeling,
Collapsing into nothingness
Trapped in a void,
There is a concern for the heart.

While the mind regresses the darkness,
A candle is lit, on the opposite side.
In a distance, far away
Hands are trying to reach out.

The meadows give solace
A minor breeze of air touching the cheeks
They stand straight, with a look in their eyes
Containing a glimpse of hope.

Human

Seeking sanctuary in a faraway land
Searching relief from fear and pain
Denied, for I was not born in the right place

Disrupt

On the edge of sanity
Insane ideas erupt
Marking a new dawn
With the purpose to disrupt

Dansk Vand

On the subject of Danish water ("Dansk Vand")

There is no argument left,
After careful consideration
And some debate,
(although still open for opinion)

Danish water tastes bleak.
Especially when compared,
To Belgium water,
Which is rich with hops
And brewed with care
And more so when compared,
To Scottish water,
Which has the flavor of malted barley,
While enriched by age in oak barrels.

There is debate on the case of health,
and no argument on the case of cheer.

We toast to our loved ones,
We toast to our friends,
We toast for peace and harmony
We toast for love and friendship
We toast to wish every dear one a good health
"Slàinte"

Voices

Once there was a time
When we had a voice,
and chose to be silent

Our silence was interpreted
And now we lost the rights,
To hear our voice again...

Yesterday & Today

Driven by progress,
Change is a constant...

Two worlds merge,
Virtual and Real

Experience the difference,
Digital and Acoustic

One world dominates,
Questions on what is real...

Existence in the balance,
The Old and the New...

Fueled by technology,
Change accelerates...

Change

Catch the wind in your hair
Standing on top of a mountain
Conquered with strength and skill
All the while, submit to it with respect

Will you understand it?
Will the forces of nature tolerate me trespassing
Will you allow it?
Will the elements be gentle to my body and soul

I climb the highest mountain
to find peace for a moment
I hike the vastest valley
to embrace my solitude for some time

I walk the curly roads
to challenge my spirit
I stroll through the fields in the rain
to feel the touch of nature

How can I not love this place...
How can I not love where I am going...
How can I not love...

A restless soul lives on and on
In search for tranquility, Some peace of mind
Closing his eyes, and finding the quietness
While resting his heart...

Dreaming Sound Asleep

Technology advances
Speed, faster, go go go
No stopping us anymore

Analogue
Signals, under pressure
Transmission in the air
Coming closer,
Remember those times
Radio waves hitting the living room
Voices and laughter,
Everywhere we listen,
Magic is surrounding us,
Emotions with people in tears

Automation
Decision, more pressure
Self-harming flow,
Humanity under control
No control, lost control
Standard view on movement
Situations being absorbed
Adapting to the now
Ignoring the then
So long, creature of faith

Robots in our sight,
March of the machines
Ignoring our needs and feeding our greed
Oh, where do we go
Loosing sense of purpose,
Is there any purpose?
So long, you miserable beast
Keep moving away,
Understanding those changes
Reflecting on those waves of the past

Hearts are drawn closer
We lost our desire
We missed our choice
We ignored the signals
Hearts became cold
Greed took it all
Leaving us behind...
Do we still have sense of purpose?
Do we still have any values?

Last Night Experience

Transmit that poem or a song
Let me hear that voice once again
Touching my heart in a moment of hope,
Penetrating my soul with sentiment, just now
Yes, I am scared, ooh yes
I tremble at the thought of walking alone

And we move on to the next...

My experience is troubled
With all the emotions running loose
Can I find some peace, right now
Some hope, presented in a touch
Yes, I am afraid, ooh yes
I tremble at the thought of feeling alone

And we move on to the next...

I walked out into the soaking rain
Experiences exchanged, surreal, real
How much time do I have to absorb this moment?
To process this flood of emotions
Yes, I feel humbled, ooh yes
I look into the lights and know that the future is bright

And we move on to the next...
Song

Do You See?

Mastering the art of receiving
Sliding the tip of a finger over the surface of a book
Feeling the words speak out...
"History in the making!

Do you see?"

A story told, a story experienced
Sucked in the narrative, wanting to see more
An adventure, drama displayed... A fantasy?
"History unfolds!

Do you see?"

Barriers

Whistle a tune for peace,
Break down those barriers,
Instead of building obstacles,
We take them down, those walls
Eventually, piece by piece

A Circumstance

Hit, a split second,
No idea what is going on...

Blackout! Down on the ground,
No airbag to soften the blow...

~~~

Probing conscious feelings, unconscious
Nursing an awareness of being,
While eyes shut, dreaming?

Wandering about, in the dark,
Overwhelmed by experience,
Drifting, searching for a way out...

Exit sign, nowhere in sight
Losing control of time,
Imprisoned in this void...

Flashing images penetrate the senses,
Searching deeper within,
Distracted by a light...
~~~

Making an inquiry into the soul
Discovery through meditation
Exploring the boundaries of the mind.

~~~

Sensing! A brief moment of awareness,
Acting! Crawling out of the darkness...

Awake! Alone in a foreign place,
Flooded by extreme feelings...

▷
~~~

No-(n)sense

Key hole view,
Restriction to find the new
Strong leg kick
Performing a dancing flick
Windowpane lost,
Hiding in the loft...

Break out move, see
Nothing to stop me to break free
Think is the notion
Perception and Ideas are in motion
True meaning found,
A journey into breaking new ground...

On Fire

A poem about the competitive nature of life and the possible
experience of a brief moment of tranquility...

Fast pace, on fire
Caught in a time bubble,
Slowing down
Looking in, looking out
Very briefly,
Experiencing the moment
On fire, returning to fast pace...

Real & Reality

(2 Verses on Existence)

Reality is ever unfinished,
It is in a state of evolution,
Never to be counted as absolute,
Always part of an evolving process...

What is real is happening,
It is a process of progression,
Measured in a moment,
Experienced with the conventions at play...

Formless

Formless to Form - Form to Formless
Some wisdom about existence...

Growing from formless to form
Experience of a beginning
Evolving from form to formless
Witness of an ending

Existence experienced in the form
Conscious mind
Existence experienced in the formless
Unknown space

Growing from form to formless
Experience of an ending
Evolving formless to form
Witness of a beginning

Closing

Walking the line of a circle may give the impression it leads you nowhere.

Walking any path in any direction may give you the impression you are heading somewhere.

By each passing of a point in the circle, wherever that point may be and by each step you take on that path, you add another tiny bit of experience to your life.

One may not be in control of everything one experiences. Each experience does leave a mark on one's life and will trigger emotions. How we process those experiences and emotions that come with them, good or bad, sad or happy, fun or bore, will determine what we do with them and how they affect our lives, negative or positive.

Life is like a learning process. It enriches us with each step we take. When we reach the end point, you realize you reached the start of a new beginning. Maybe a circle to a presumed nowhere or a path to somewhere...

About the Author

Peinsejoager was born in Ghent (Belgium) and currently lives in the countryside in Denmark.

Peinsejoager has a blog about things (peinsejoager.blog). The philosophy behind the blog is simple. Subjects for the blog are poached from the author's own experience and the world. They are used to make aware and hopefully sometimes entertain people in the form of poems. Subjects poached are not necessarily wanted or desired. They are an expression of free thinking where reason, emotions and feelings are the prime drivers.

Peinsejoager is a dialect word from Ghent – Belgium that translates in English to poacher.

"Once more the sun rises
Starting another peaceful day in paradise,
We are grateful to be here,
Walking these fields
and enjoy the feeling to be free..."